HOW DOES IT MOVE?
FORCES AND MOTION

HOW DOES LIGHT MOVE?

JAN MADER

Cavendish Square
New York

Published in 2019 by Cavendish Square Publishing, LLC
243 5th Avenue, Suite 136, New York, NY 10016

Copyright © 2019 by Cavendish Square Publishing, LLC

First Edition

No part of this publication may be reproduced, stored in a retrieval system, or transmitted in any form or by any means–electronic, mechanical, photocopying, recording, or otherwise–without the prior permission of the copyright owner. Request for permission should be addressed to Permissions, Cavendish Square Publishing, 243 5th Avenue, Suite 136, New York, NY 10016. Tel (877) 980-4450; fax (877) 980-4454.

Website: cavendishsq.com

This publication represents the opinions and views of the author based on his or her personal experience, knowledge, and research. The information in this book serves as a general guide only. The author and publisher have used their best efforts in preparing this book and disclaim liability rising directly or indirectly from the use and application of this book.

All websites were available and accurate when this book was sent to press.

Library of Congress Cataloging-in-Publication Data

Names: Mader, Jan (Janet G), author.
Title: How does light move? / Jan Mader.
Description: First edition. | New York : Cavendish Square Publishing, [2019] |
Series: How does it move? Forces and motion |
Includes bibliographical references and index. | Audience: 2-5.
Identifiers: LCCN 2017053337 (print) | LCCN 2017059635 (ebook) |
ISBN 9781502637826 (ebook) | ISBN 9781502637796 | ISBN 9781502637796 (library bound) | ISBN 9781502637802(pbk.) | ISBN 9781502637819 (6 pack)
Subjects: LCSH: Light–Juvenile literature.
Classification: LCC QC360 (ebook) | LCC QC360 .M33 2019 (print) | DDC 535–dc23
LC record available at https://lccn.loc.gov/2017053337

Editorial Director: David McNamara
Editor: Meghan Lamb
Copy Editor: Michele Suchomel-Casey
Associate Art Director: Amy Greenan
Designer: Megan Mette
Production Coordinator: Karol Szymczuk
Photo Research: J8 Media

The photographs in this book are used by permission and through the courtesy of: Cover Jose A. Bernat Bacete/Moment Select/Getty Images; p. 4 Jupiterimages/The Image Bank/Getty Images; p. 7 Jan Baumann/Stock4B/Getty Images; p. 8 OGI75/Shutterstock.com; p. 9 Mary Hockenbery/Moment/Getty Images; p. 10 Photo Researchers/Science History Images/Alamy Stock Photo; p. 11 JTB/UIG/Getty Images; p. 12 Kelly Sillaste/Moment Select/Getty Images; p. 15 Siarhei Dzmitryienka/Shutterstock.com; p. 16 Photo Researchers/Science Source/Getty Images; p. 18 Esbeauda/Shutterstock.com; p. 19 Biletskiy_Evgeniy/iStock/Thinkstock.com; p. 20 Dr T J Martin/Moment Open/Getty Images; p. 21 Alex Zotov/Shutterstock.com; p. 22 Howard Roberts/EyeEm/Getty Images; p. 24 Yon Marsh/Alamy Stock Photo; p. 25 Tornado Design/Shutterstock.com; p. 26 William Whitehurst/Corbis/Getty Images.

Printed in the United States of America

CONTENTS

1 What Is Light? 5

2 How Light Moves 13

3 The Discovery of Light 23

How Does It Move Quiz 28

Glossary 29

Find Out More 30

Index 31

About the Author 32

When a flashlight is turned on, a beam of light shines out.

CHAPTER 1

WHAT IS LIGHT?

Some things make their own **light**, but most do not. The sun lights up Earth. The sun is a natural source of light. The sun **reflects** off things we can see, like cars and clouds.

There is **artificial** light, too. People use lamps to see the words in a book. Lamps are artificial lights.

Have you ever turned on a flashlight in a tent at night? Have you ever watched the small, bright circle move as you moved the flashlight? It probably looked strange as it moved through the dark. It probably felt like magic.

Light may feel like magic, but it is really made up of energy. **Energy** is how things change or more. A **wave** is a motion that travels through space. It transfers energy to other things. Think about a wave in the ocean. It ripples out and moves away. Light waves do the same thing. They move away from one place to another. The sun sends energy in the form of light.

Each ray of light moves in a wave. These waves allow light to move very fast. Light travels at 186,000 miles (299,338 kilometers) per second.

Let's think back to that flashlight in the tent. Imagine the glow from your flashlight. Light from a flashlight moves around a tent the second it's turned on. You move the flashlight from left to right. Light hits the objects in the tent. The objects **reflect** the light.

These children can see the beam of light as it travels from their flashlights to the tent.

WAYS LIGHT MOVES

Light moves in different ways. It bounces. It bends. Sometimes, light even looks like it is breaking. Let's take a closer look at the ways light moves!

Picture a mirror like the one you have on the bathroom wall. A mirror is flat and smooth. A mirror

Light hits the mirror and bounces back so the boy can see his face. This process is called refraction.

reflects light. You can see your face in a mirror. That's because light from your face refracts off the mirror.

When the light waves **refract**, they may appear to bend. Light waves refract when they move from one source to another. Refracted light seems to bounce. It is almost like a ball that bounces off the blacktop on a playground.

Curved mirrors can reflect light, too. If a mirror curves out, it makes you look tall. If a mirror curves in, it makes you look short. Have you ever seen a curved mirror at a fair? It is fun to stand and look at yourself. You can make yourself look tall and skinny. You can make yourself look short and fat.

Here is an easy experiment that will show how light refracts. First, pour water into a

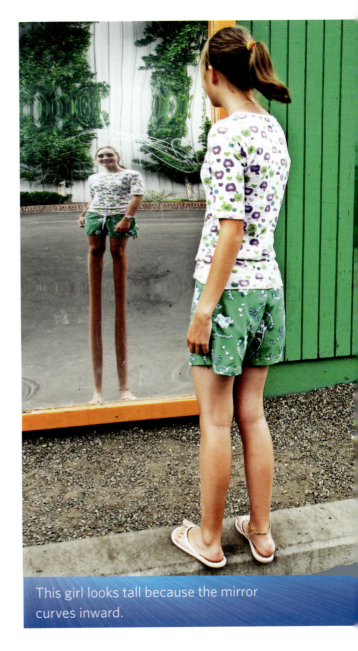

This girl looks tall because the mirror curves inward.

clear glass until the glass is half full. Next, put a spoon inside of the glass. Does the spoon look like it breaks where the water hits it?

The spoon is not really broken. Refraction makes the spoon look broken. Light bends as it hits the water in the glass.

This happens because water and glass are **transparent**. Transparent means see-through. Objects look like they bend or break where they meet a transparent surface.

The spoon is not really broken. Light bends as it hits the water in the glass.

BEAMS OF SUNLIGHT

Sunlight **beams** are often seen at dawn and at dusk. A beam is a ray of light. These beams happen when objects **shadow** and scatter the rays from the sun. Clouds can shadow the sunbeams. A shadow is something that blocks light. Tree branches can block light. Tree branches can also scatter light.

The rays of light from the sun produce beautiful sunbeams.

These red boots reflect from water on a playground.

CHAPTER 2

HOW LIGHT MOVES

You probably look at yourself in a mirror every day. Have you ever looked at yourself in water? Water acts like a mirror when light hits it. When you look at the water, you can see your reflection.

You can see a reflection of your face when light bounces off of a mirror. The same thing happens when you look in a clear pool of water. It happens when you look into a store window. Why? Because light bounces off an object. You are that object!

The water shows your reflection. Light bounces off of flat objects. The mirror is a smooth and shiny surface. The light that hits the mirror reflects back at the same angle. That allows you to see your reflection.

When light bounces off a rough object, your image is not as clear. You can see your reflection in a metal slide, but it is wavy or rough. Try looking at your reflection in other metal objects. How clear are they?

When light hits a flat surface, it bounces off. When light rays hit a smooth surface, they reflect in the same direction. When light rays hit a rough surface, they reflect in different directions. That is why your reflection in a metal slide is not as clear.

Let's think back to our experiment with the spoon in the glass of water. Did the part of the spoon that touched the water look different? It probably looked

WE NEED LIGHT TO LIVE

The sun is our most important source of light. Only a tiny amount of light ever gets to Earth. But it's enough light that it is possible for everything to live. Plants and trees could not live without sunlight. They would not grow. When people need more light they make up artificial light. People use lightbulbs to light up rooms when it's dark.

Almost everything on Earth needs sunlight to live.

Light looks different when it travels from air to water.

broken or bent. It probably looked a little thicker.

Objects look different when light travels from the air into the water. Light slows down when it hits the water. This makes the light change directions just a bit. The light changes directions because it bends, or refracts.

DIFFERENT KINDS OF LIGHT

Let's try another experiment with light.

16　HOW DOES LIGHT MOVE?

Take a flashlight into a dark room. Shine your flashlight onto the dark wall and watch the area light up. Now, move your hand in front of the flashlight. Look at the wall. You should see the shadow of your hand moving across the lighted area.

When you put your hand in front of the flashlight, it blocks the light. The light that isn't on the wall is on your hand!

There are two different kinds of light. One kind of light is visible. That means you can see it. The other kind of light is invisible. That means you cannot see it. The sun gives off **ultraviolet** light. We can't see that light but it's the kind of light that gives us a sunburn!

Have you ever seen a rainbow after a storm? You can see all the colors of visible light in a rainbow. A rainbow is red, orange, yellow, green, blue, indigo, and violet. These colors are visible light. Isn't the rainbow beautiful?

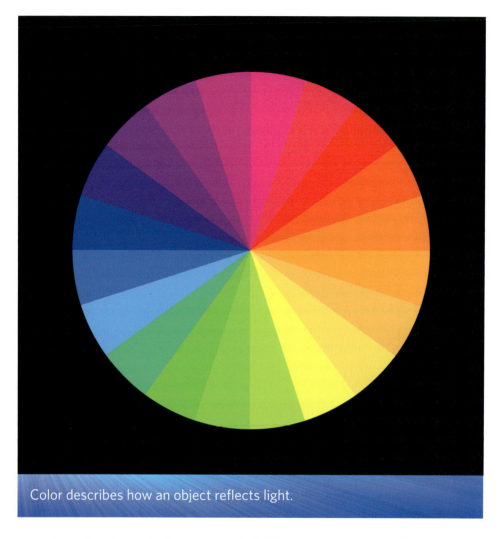

Color describes how an object reflects light.

How is the rainbow made? The answer is refraction. The sunlight shines through the water droplets in the air. The light bends or refracts as it passes though the water droplets. The refracted sunlight forms an arch. It shows all of the colors of the light.

Light travels along straight lines. We call these lines rays. You can see them when the sun shines through

Rainbows are created when light refracts through water.

When a ray of light enters a raindrop, it refracts.

a break in the clouds. Remember that light rays move almost like an ocean wave.

In chapter 1, we learned that light moves in waves. These waves move in arches like rainbows. The high

FAST FACT

Some people think dogs cannot see colors. They are wrong. Dogs can see yellows and blues. Their vision isn't as good as ours, but they can see motion better than we do!

points of the arch are called **peaks**. The low points of the arch are called **valleys**. The space between two peaks or two valleys is called the **wavelength**. The wavelength is what we use to measure light waves.

This dog can see the yellow and blue parts of the rainbow.

A prism separates light that passes through it into different colors.

CHAPTER 3

THE DISCOVERY OF LIGHT

We see beautiful colors around us every day. Light is something we might not think about much. A long time ago scientists wondered about light. Light looks white, so where do the colors come from?

Sir Isaac Newton was a famous scientist. Once, he thought that white light was all white. Then, he began to experiment with light. He used a prism. A prism is

The prism breaks the white light into different colors.

usually a piece of glass or plastic. Material like that refracts light. Prisms are usually shaped like a triangle. When light goes through a prism something amazing happens. The prism breaks the white light into different colors!

Isaac Newton looked into the prism. He was amazed by what he saw. The white light was actually made of many different colors. It was made of red, orange, yellow, green, blue, and purple.

MAKE YOUR OWN RAINBOW

You can make your own rainbow! You will need a flashlight, a sink, and white paper. First turn down the lights. Then turn on the faucet. Shine your flashlight against the piece of paper. Now move so the flashlight beam goes through the stream of water. Your white paper will catch the rainbow!

You can use a flashlight and water to make your own rainbow.

You made a rainbow because the running water was like a prism and mirror. It separated the colors and reflected them onto your white paper.

THE DISCOVERY OF LIGHT   25

PRISMS AND RAINBOWS

Now, Isaac Newton knew that light was not just white. He saw that the light bent as it passed through the

Diamonds are like prisms because they refract light. All these beautiful colors came from the refracted light.

prism. He saw that each color bent at a different angle. The white light separates into all colors of the rainbow.

Have you ever seen someone wearing a diamond ring? Diamonds are like prisms because they refract light. Light refracts when it shines on the different sides of the diamond. Diamonds sparkle with different colors from the refracted light.

Light can be controlled and made in many ways. We use light in our televisions. We use flashlights and nightlights. We use light in our homes and schools.

FAST FACT

A long time ago, people did not have electric light. When the sky was clear, they used sunlight and moonlight to see. They used fire outside and inside. They made candles to use inside.

Today, we flip a switch and have light. We can read, watch TV, and use our computers. It is hard to think about our lives without light!

HOW DOES IT MOVE QUIZ

Question 1: What do light waves do when they refract?

Question 2: What is it called when you see yourself in the mirror?

Question 3: What did Sir Isaac Newton see when he looked into a prism?

Answer 3: A rainbow

Answer 2: A reflection

Answer 1: They bend away from a straight line.

GLOSSARY

artificial *Made by human skill or something produced by humans.*

beam *A ray or shaft of light.*

energy *The ability for light to perform work.*

light *Something that makes things visible; the illumination from a particular source.*

peak *The highest point of anything.*

reflect *To cast back light from a smooth surface.*

refract *When a light ray is bent away from a straight path.*

shadow *A dark shape that appears on a surface when something blocks the light.*

transparent *See-through.*

ultraviolet *Rays of light that cannot be seen.*

valley *A low point or level point.*

wave *A motion that travels through space.*

wavelength *The distance between two peaks or valleys.*

FIND OUT MORE

BOOKS

Clark, John E. *The Basics of Light. New York, NY: Rosen Publishing Group, Inc, 2015.*

Kopp, Megan. *Light Works. New York, NY: AV2 by Weigl, 2012*

WEBSITES

National Geographic Kids

https://kids.nationalgeographic.com/explore/science/lightning-/#lightning-trees.jpg

Kids get to see how fast light moves as they watch lightning strike.

PBS Learning Media

http://bit.ly/2yXUmYd

Sid the Science Kid teaches students all about light and its sources.

INDEX

Page numbers in **boldface** are illustrations.

artificial light, 5, 15, 27

beams, 11, **11**

color, 17, **18**, 19, 23–25, 27

diamonds, **26**, 27

Earth, 5, 15

energy, 6

flashlight, **4**, 5–6, **7**, 17, 25, 27

invisible light, 17

mirror, 7–8, **8**, **9**, 13

Newton, Isaac, 23–24, 26

peaks, 21

prism, **22**, 23–25, **24**, 27

rainbow, 17–20, **19**, 25, **25**, 27

rays, 14, 19–10

reflection, 5–6, 8–9, **12**, 13–14, 25

refraction, 8–10, 16, 18–19, **20**, 24

shadow, 11, 17

sun, 5, 11, **11**, 15, **15**, 17–18, 27

transparent, 10

ultraviolet, 17

valleys, 21

visible light, 17

water, 9–10, **10**, 13–14, 16, **16**, 18–19

wave, 6, 20–21

wavelength, 21

ABOUT THE AUTHOR

Jan Mader has written many books for children. Her books can be found in classrooms and libraries around the world. Jan has been an educator for over 20 years. She began her writing career to meet the needs of the students in her classroom.